KING MEDHAVI HAD NO CHILDREN. HE PRAYED TO LORD VISHNU TO GRANT HIM A SON. HIS PRAYER WAS HEARD AND THE QUEEN GAVE BIRTH TO A BABY BOY.

A MONTH LATER—

MAHARAJ! OUR ENEMIES HAVE SURROUNDED THE FORT!

RALLY OUR MEN. WE WILL GIVE THEM A FITTING REPLY.

IN THE FIERCE BATTLE THAT FOLLOWED, MEDHAVI WAS KILLED.

WHEN THE NEWS OF HIS DEATH REACHED THE QUEEN—

NO! NO! MY SON!

OH, MY DARLING SON, I MUST JOIN YOUR FATHER. MAY LORD VISHNU PROTECT YOU FROM HARM.

THEN SHE SENT FOR HER OLD NURSE.

I ENTRUST MY SON TO YOU. TAKE HIM AND FLEE.

THE PRINCE IS SAFE WITH ME. I SHALL PROTECT HIM AS LONG AS I LIVE.

AS WAS THE CUSTOM IN THOSE DAYS, THE QUEEN OBSERVED SATI.*

MEANWHILE —

GO OUT THROUGH THAT TUNNEL. BE QUICK.

*A WIDOW JOINING HER HUSBAND ON THE FUNERAL PYRE.

THE FAITHFUL OLD NURSE TOOK THE PRINCE TO KUNTALA, A DISTANT TOWN.

HERE'S SOME FOOD FOR YOUR GRANDSON.

MAY GOD BLESS YOU, MOTHER.

WHAT A FATE! WERE YOU BORN A PRINCE ONLY TO LIVE ON ALMS?

WHEN THE PRINCE WAS FIVE YEARS OLD, THE NURSE DIED.

MA, GET UP. GET UP, MA, I'M HUNGRY.

AFTER THAT THE WOMEN OF THE NEIGHBOUR-HOOD FED THE ENDEARING ORPHAN PRINCE.

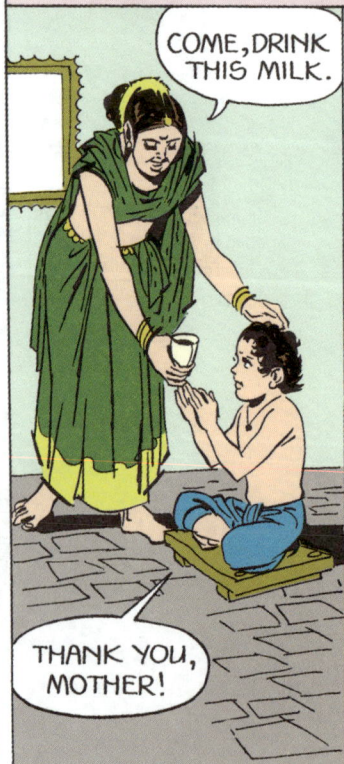

COME, DRINK THIS MILK.

THANK YOU, MOTHER!

I'M HUNGRY, MOTHER.

HERE IS A JUICY MANGO FOR YOU.

ONE DAY—

I TOO WOULD LIKE TO PLAY.

LORD VISHNU, I WANT A MARBLE. PLEASE GIVE ME ONE.

THE NEXT DAY—

MAY I JOIN YOU, PLEASE?

ONLY IF YOU HAVE A MARBLE.

AH, A MARBLE!

WHAT THE ORPHAN PRINCE DID NOT KNOW WAS THAT IT WAS A SHALAGRAM.*

* A BLACK STONE, USUALLY ROUND IN SHAPE, CONSIDERED TO BE A REPRESENTATION OF VISHNU.

FROM THEN ON THE BOY'S LUCK TURNED. HE ALWAYS WON WITH HIS BLACK MARBLE. THE BOYS ADMIRED HIM AND...

...VERY SOON HE BECAME THEIR LEADER.

COME ON, BOYS.

THOUGH THE ORPHAN PRINCE HAD NEITHER HOME NOR FAMILY HE WAS THE HAPPIEST BOY IN THE NEIGHBOURHOOD.

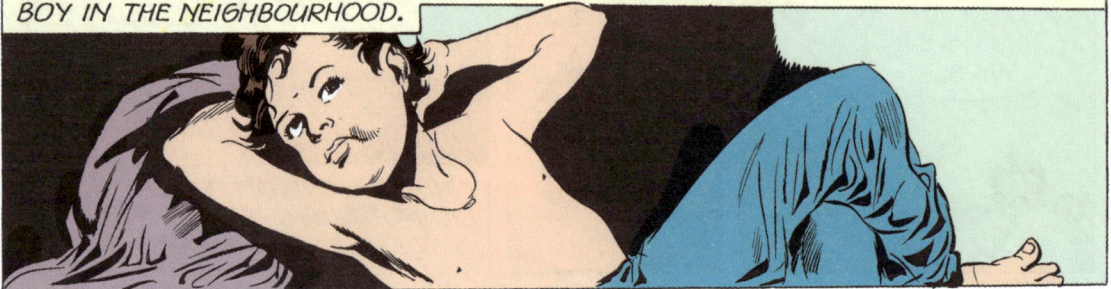

ONE DAY, THE ORPHAN PRINCE AND HIS GANG WERE PLAYING IN FRONT OF THE HOUSE OF DUSHTABUDDHI, THE CHIEF MINISTER OF KUNTALA, WHO WAS SEEING OFF HIS GUEST, A LEARNED BRAHMAN. WHEN THE BRAHMAN SAW THE PRINCE —

WHO IS THAT BOY, DUSHTABUDDHI?

A STREET URCHIN, I SUPPOSE. WHY DO YOU ASK?

MARK MY WORDS. ONE DAY HE WILL BE THE KING OF KUNTALA. TAKE HIM UNDER YOUR CARE AND GIVE HIM A PROPER EDUCATION.

THE KING OF KUNTALA! HM.. M..M..M!

MADANA, MY SON — NOT THIS URCHIN — SHALL BE THE KING OF KUNTALA.

DUSHTABUDDHI HAD DESIGNS ON THE THRONE OF KUNTALA FOR THE KING HAD NO SON.

I MUST ACT FAST.

SOON AFTERWARDS —

DO YOU SEE THAT BOY IN THE CENTRE?

YES, I DO.

SO DO I.

TAKE HIM TO THE FOREST AND KILL HIM. YOU WILL BE WELL REWARDED.

LEAVE IT TO US, SIR. WE WILL DO THE JOB.

RUN!

RUN!

THEY MEAN TO KILL US!

YOU ARE THE ONE WE WANT.

WHERE ARE YOU TAKING ME?

HA! HA! HA!

TO THE HOUSE OF YAMA.*

*GOD OF DEATH

THE KILLERS TOOK THE BOY TO THE FOREST.

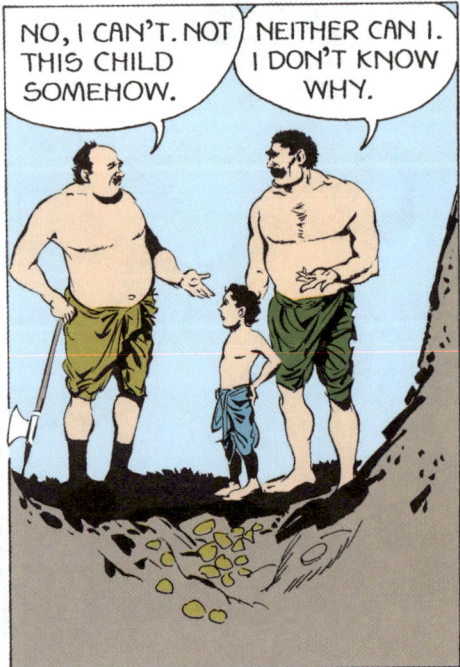

I'LL HOLD HIM. YOU CUT OFF HIS HEAD.

HARI, HARI.*

I WILL HOLD HIM. YOU DO THE KILLING.

ALL RIGHT. I WILL.

HARI. HARI.

NO, I CAN'T. NOT THIS CHILD SOMEHOW.

NEITHER CAN I. I DON'T KNOW WHY.

* ANOTHER NAME OF LORD VISHNU

10

LET'S HOPE THE JACKALS HAVE A FINE FEAST.

BUT THE PRINCE WAS VERY MUCH ALIVE. HE WAS BEING CARED FOR BY THE ANIMALS OF THE FOREST.

ONE DAY, KALINDAKA OF CHANDANAVATI, A VASSAL OF THE KING OF KUNTALA, CAME TO THAT FOREST TO HUNT.

12

WHEN HE SAW THE BOY—

WHAT ARE YOU DOING HERE ALONE, MY CHILD? WHOSE SON ARE YOU?

I HAVE NO FATHER OR MOTHER...

...AND I DON'T HAVE A SON.

FROM NOW ON I SHALL BE YOUR FATHER AND YOU, MY SON.

AND KING KALINDAKA TOOK THE ORPHAN PRINCE TO HIS PALACE.

LATER — WHEN THIS CHILD SMILES, IT SEEMS AS THOUGH THE WHOLE PLACE IS FLOODED WITH MOONLIGHT.

AH, MY QUEEN, YOU HAVE JUST GIVEN HIM HIS NAME. WE WILL CALL HIM CHANDRAHASA.*

O VENERABLE ONE, I LEAVE CHANDRAHASA IN YOUR CARE. PLEASE TEACH HIM ALL THAT A PRINCE SHOULD KNOW.

"CHANDRA" MOON
HASA = SMILE

UNDER THE GUIDANCE OF HIS TEACHER, CHANDRAHASA SOON BECAME AN EXPERT IN THE USE OF WEAPONS...

...AND IN STATECRAFT.

WHEN HE WAS EIGHTEEN YEARS OLD, KING KALINDAKA FORMALLY INSTALLED CHANDRAHASA AS HIS SUCCESSOR.

A FEW DAYS LATER, KALINDAKA SENT FOR CHANDRAHASA.

DUSHTABUDDHI, THE CHIEF MINISTER OF KUNTALA WILL BE VISITING US. I WANT YOU TO RECEIVE HIM.

AS YOU WISH, FATHER.

WELCOME TO CHANDANA-VATI, SIR.

LATER —

KALINDAKA, WHO WAS THAT YOUNG OFFICER WHO RECEIVED ME AT THE MAIN ENTRANCE?

IT WAS MY SON, CHANDRAHASA.

YOUR SON? BUT YOU DON'T HAVE A SON. HOW DID YOU COME BY THIS ONE?

SOME THIRTEEN YEARS AGO I FOUND HIM ALONE IN THE FOREST. I ADOPTED HIM.

THIRTEEN YEARS AGO? CHANDRAHASA CAN BE NONE OTHER THAN THAT STREET URCHIN. THE KILLERS MUST HAVE DECEIVED ME. WILL THE PREDICTION COME TRUE? NOT IF I CAN HELP IT.

DUSHTABUDDHI IMMEDIATELY HATCHED ANOTHER PLOT TO KILL CHANDRAHASA.

CHANDRAHASA, YOU ARE A DEPENDABLE YOUNG MAN. RIDE TO KUNTALA AND GIVE MY SON, MADANA, THIS LETTER. IT IS HIGHLY CONFIDENTIAL.

IT IS MY PRIVILEGE TO BE OF SERVICE TO YOU, SIR.

CHANDRAHASA RODE AS FAST AS HE COULD, TOWARDS KUNTALA.

ON THE OUTSKIRTS OF THE CITY, HE SAW A BEAUTIFUL GARDEN.

HE SUDDENLY REALISED THAT HE WAS TIRED.

I MAY AS WELL REST HERE FOR A WHILE.

HE WAS SO TIRED THAT HE SOON FELL FAST ASLEEP.

JUST THEN, DUSHTABUDDHI'S BEAUTIFUL DAUGHTER, VISHAYA, CAME TO THE GARDEN.

AS THEY WERE GATHERING FLOWERS, SHE STRAYED AWAY FROM HER FRIENDS. SUDDENLY SHE CHANCED TO SEE THE PRINCE.

HOW HANDSOME HE IS! WHO COULD HE BE? HE HAS A LETTER WITH HIM!

THE LETTER! THE LETTER WILL SURELY REVEAL HIS IDENTITY.

OVERCOME BY CURIOSITY SHE TOOK IT...

...AND READ IT.

DEAR MADANA, THE BEARER OF THIS LETTER IS DESTINED TO BECOME THE KING OF KUNTALA. THEREFORE, WITHOUT WAITING FOR MY RETURN, GIVE HIM VISHA*

VISHA? THERE MUST BE SOME MISTAKE. I KNOW... IN HIS HURRY FATHER HAS MIS-SPELT MY NAME.

21

OH, HOW KIND AND THOUGHTFUL OF FATHER! WHAT A HANDSOME MAN HE HAS CHOSEN FOR ME.

BUT WILL MADANA UNDERSTAND THAT THE WORD IS VISHAYA AND NOT VISHA?

SUPPOSE HE TAKES IT TO BE VISHA AND POISONS HIM. OH GOD, NO!

USING A STALK AND HER KAAJAL* SHE ADDED "YA" TO VISHA.

...GIVE HIM VISHAYA.

*A GREASY BLACK EYE COSMETIC.

22

PLEASED WITH HERSELF, SHE REPLACED THE LETTER AND WALKED QUIETLY AWAY.

HOW FORTUNATE THAT I READ THE LETTER!

THAT EVENING —

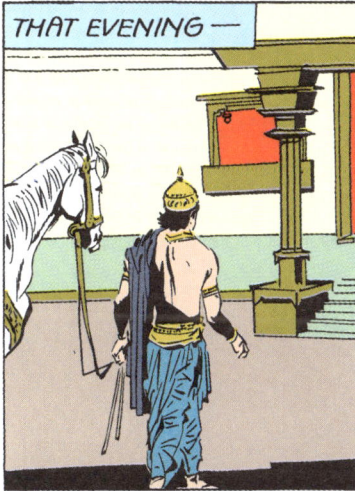

YOU MUST BE MADANA. I HAVE A LETTER FOR YOU FROM YOUR FATHER.

VISHAYA, FATHER HAS FOUND MANMATHA* HIMSELF FOR YOU.

SINCE DUSHTABUDDHI HAD NEVER CONFIDED IN HIS SON, MADANA SAW NOTHING STRANGE IN HIS FATHER'S ORDERS.

*THE HINDU GOD OF LOVE.

23

SO CHANDRAHASA WAS SOON MARRIED TO VISHAYA.

DUSHTABUDDHI RETURNED A FEW DAYS LATER.

BLESS US, FATHER.

YOU FOOL! WHY DID YOU DISOBEY ME?

I...I... DON'T UNDERSTAND. I HAVE OBEYED YOU TO THE LAST LETTER FATHER.

GIVE HIM VISHAYA...

IMPOSSIBLE! HOW DID I MAKE SUCH A MISTAKE?

THEN DUSHTABUDDHI MADE A CRUEL DECISION.

CHANDRAHASA SHALL DIE EVEN IF IT MAKES MY DAUGHTER A WIDOW.

MADANA, ASK CHANDRAHASA TO SEE ME.

AS YOU WISH FATHER.

I WANT YOU TO VISIT THE TEMPLE OF KALI TONIGHT AND OFFER WORSHIP TO THE MOTHER.

THAT I WILL FATHER, GLADLY.

MEANWHILE, THE OLD KING OF KUNTALA SENT FOR THE ROYAL PRIEST.

WHEN I LOOKED INTO THE MIRROR, I SAW A HEADLESS REFLECTION OF MY BODY. WHAT DOES THAT MEAN, REVERED SIR?

IT SIGNIFIES THAT YOUR END IS DRAWING NEAR. O KING, THINK OF SHRI HARI IN YOUR LAST DAYS ON EARTH.

BUT SIR, MY BELOVED DAUGHTER IS NOT YET MARRIED.

DON'T DESPAIR, O KING. WHY DON'T YOU MARRY YOUR DAUGHTER, TOO, TO CHANDRAHASA, THE NOBLE SON-IN-LAW OF DUSHTABUDDHI?

A GOOD PROPOSAL. SEND FOR HIM AT ONCE, SIR.

MADANA, WHERE IS CHANDRAHASA? THE KING WOULD LIKE TO SEE HIM, IMMEDIATELY.

I'LL GO AND TELL HIM, SIR.

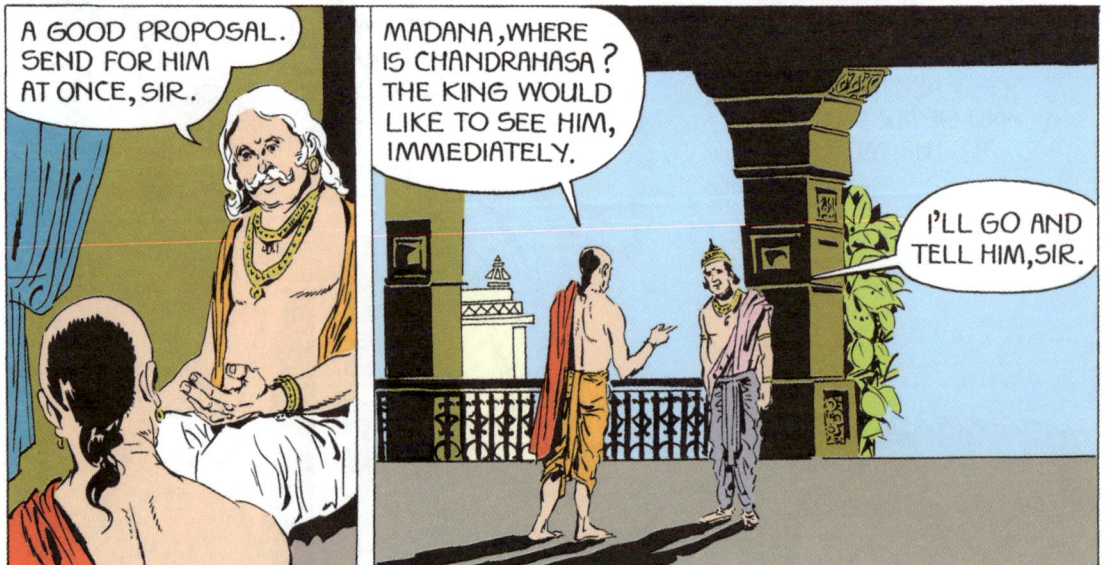

27

AS SOON AS CHANDRAHASA REACHED THE PALACE, HE WAS MARRIED TO THE PRINCESS.

SOON AFTER, HE WAS CROWNED KING OF KUNTALA.

THEN CHANDRAHASA AND HIS SECOND BRIDE VISITED DUSHTABUDDHI.

BLESS US, FATHER.

CHANDRAHASA, WHY HAVEN'T YOU GONE TO THE TEMPLE?

THE KING SENT FOR ME. SO MADANA WENT IN MY PLACE, SIR.

WHAT! MADANA GONE TO THE TEMPLE! OH! GOD! NO!

DUSHTABUDDHI HURRIED TO THE TEMPLE, RUNNING AS FAST AS HE COULD.

GOD, LET ME BE THERE IN TIME TO SAVE MY SON!

BUT HE WAS TOO LATE. THE KILLERS, WHO WERE ORDERED BY HIM TO KILL THE LONELY YOUNG WORSHIPPER VISITING THE TEMPLE THAT EVENING, HAD KILLED MADANA, WHO HAD GONE THERE IN PLACE OF CHANDRAHASA.

OVERCOME BY GRIEF AND REPENTANCE, DUSHTABUDDHI STABBED HIMSELF.

A FEW MINUTES LATER, CHANDRAHASA TOO CAME THERE.

MOTHER KALI, DUSHTABUDDHI HAS PAID FOR HIS SINS WITH HIS OWN LIFE. PLEASE BRING HIM AND THE INNO-CENT MADANA BACK TO LIFE. MOTHER, HAVE MERCY ON THEM.

WHEN HIS PRAYER REMAINED UNHEARD —

THEN ACCEPT MY LIFE, MOTHER KALI, AND LET THE FATHER AND SON LIVE.

JUST THEN —

WAIT! I WILL NOT ALLOW ONE LIKE YOU TO DIE. I'LL BRING THEM BACK TO LIFE.

I HAVE SINNED GREATLY AGAINST YOU, CHANDRAHASA; FORGIVE ME.

BUT FATHER! YOUR SIN HAS ALREADY BEEN WASHED AWAY BY YOUR BLOOD. YOU ARE A NEW MAN NOW. COME, LET US RETURN HOME.

CHANDRAHASA RULED OVER KUNTALA AND CHANDANAVATI AND LIVED HAPPILY WITH HIS TWO WIVES.

THE ACK QUIZ

EPICS & MYTHOLOGY

1 Which god rides a crow?

2 Name Surya's charioteer.

3 Who are the two brothers in the image?

4 Which kingdom are they fighting for?

5 Which of these two brothers was an ally of Rama?

6 What is the name of Indra's weapo[n]

7 What is the name of his elephant[?]

8 What is the name of Indra's capit[al]

9 Who is the guru of the asuras?

10 The gods and asuras churned the ocean for _____.